# Rosie & Jim
## A Family for Duck

**By John Cunliffe   Illustrated by Joan Hickson**

A Ragdoll Production for Central Independent Television

Hippo

Scholastic Children's Books,
Scholastic Publications Ltd,
7-9 Pratt Street, London NW1 0AE, UK

Scholastic Inc.,
555 Broadway, New York, NY 10012-3999,
USA

Scholastic Canada Ltd,
123 Newkirk Road, Richmond Hill,
Ontario, Canada L4C 3G5

Ashton Scholastic Pty Ltd,
PO Box 579, Gosford, New South Wales,
Australia

Ashton Scholastic Ltd
Private Bag 92801, Penrose, Auckland,
New Zealand

First published by Scholastic Publications Ltd, 1993

Text copyright © John Cunliffe, 1993
Illustrations copyright © Joan Hickson, 1993

Based on the Central Independent Television series
produced by Ragdoll Productions

ISBN 0 590 54101 3

Typeset by Rapid Reprographics
Printed in Hong Kong by the Paramount Printing Group

All rights reserved

10 9 8 7 6

"Look !" said Jim.

"Baby ducks!" said Rosie.

"Quack," said Duck.

"What a lovely family of ducklings,"
said John looking over the side of
the *Ragdoll*. He was on his way
again, looking out for new stories.

3

"Quack!" said Duck again.

"Duck sounds sad," said Rosie.

"He is," said Jim. "He wants some babies of his own."

"Oh, noggin," said Rosie, "poor old Duck."

"Let's help him," said Jim.

"Great idea," said Rosie. "Wait until John goes off and then we'll see..."

John steered the boat through two locks, then tied up in the canal-basin, where there was a shop. He went off with his shopping-bag.

Duck quacked to tell Rosie and Jim.
They popped out of the hatch.

"Come on, noggin Duck," said
Rosie, "we're off to find you some
babies."

"Rosie?" said Jim. "Where are we going to look?"

"Ooooh, noodle," said Rosie, "there are babies everywhere. Babies in the trees. Babies in the grass. Babies in the water."

"Look," said Jim. "There are some baby ducks, swimming in the water!"

"Silly noggin," said Rosie. "He can't have her babies. He has to find his own."

"Well," said Jim, "let's look in the field over there. I can see lots of babies there."

Rosie and Jim climbed the stile into the field.

There were some lambs in the field.
"They look nice babies," said Jim,
"come and see."

They walked across the fields to see the lambs. There were some sheep behind the hedge. They pushed through a gap in the hedge. They butted at Jim with their horns and chased him away.

"Oh, noggin!" said Rosie. "Duck can't have lambs for his babies."

"The sheep are their mums," said Jim.

"Never mind," said Rosie. "We'll look somewhere else."

Rosie and Jim walked to the farm. There were some piglets rooting about in the yard.

"Look," said Jim. "More babies."

"They don't look a bit like ducks," said Rosie.

There was a calf in the barn.
"Too big," said Jim.

There were some kittens by the
kitchen door. "Too scratchy," said
Rosie. "And I don't think they can
swim."

"*Where* can Duck find some babies?" said Jim.

"I don't know, gobbin," said Rosie.

"Let's go and see what John's doing," said Jim.

They set out, back to the canal.
The sun was going down.

"It's too late to find a baby for
Duck, now," said Jim.

"Poor old Duck," said Rosie, "he'll
be so sad when we tell him."

"There are so many ducks in the canal," said Rosie.

"But none like our Duck," said Jim.

"I wonder if John knows," said Rosie, "where Duck can find a baby."

"Quick," said Jim, "here he comes!"

John sat down to write his story.

"What is he going to write about today?" said Rosie to herself.

"Is he going to write about babies?" said Jim to himself.

Then John smiled. He had remembered what was in his shopping-bag. What could it be? It was something that made funny bulging and sticking-out shapes in its wrapping-paper.

John unwrapped his shopping.

"Oh!" said Rosie.

"Oh!" said Jim.

They were two little wooden ducks.

"Lovely," said John. "Just like Duck. Two baby ducks. Now that could be my story for today..."

Rosie and Jim nudged each other and laughed with joy.

"Just what Duck wants," said Rosie. "Two little wooden baby ducks."

"But," said Jim.

"What?" said Rosie

"They're not coloured like *our* Duck."

"When John goes to sleep..." said Rosie.

"We'll get our paints out..." said Jim.

"And paint them!" said Rosie.

"Great!" said Jim.

"Fizzy," said Rosie.

"Now then, Duck," said Rosie.

"No quacking," said Jim.

"We've found you two babies," said Rosie.

"Take good care of them," said Jim.

23

"Feathery ducks on the water,"
said Jim.
"And wooden ducks on the boat,"
said Rosie.

"The babies are like their mums
and dads," said Jim.

"But smaller," said Rosie.

"And louder, and splashier," said Jim

"Not the wooden ones," said
Rosie.
    "They're all happy," said Jim.
    "So they are," said Rosie.

"My goodness!" said John. "How did the little ducks get there? I think my Duck wants them for his own. And...I do believe they have changed colour.

Now they are just like my good old Duck. He looks really proud of them, just as though they were his babies."

"Well, that's a nice idea," said
John. "A family for Duck. That's
what comes of writing a story
about them."

"We helped, after all, didn't we?"
said Jim.

"Of course we did, Fizzpot," said
Rosie.

"We always do," said Jim.